D0297251

FIVE FORGET MOTHER'S DAY

Other adventures in this series:

Enid Blyton

FIVE FORGET MOTHER'S DAY

Text by
Bruno Vincent

Enid Blyton for Grown-Ups

Quercus

First published in Great Britain in 2017 by

Quercus Editions Ltd
Carmelite House
50 Victoria Embankment
London EC4Y 0DZ

An Hachette UK company

A CIP catalogue record for this book is available
from the British Library

HB ISBN 978 1 78648 686 8

Text by Bruno Vincent
Original illustrations by Eileen A. Soper
Cover illustration by Ruth Palmer

10 9 8 7 6 5 4 3 2 1

Typeset by CC Book Production

Printed and bound in Great Britain by Clays Ltd, St Ives plc

Contents

CHAPTER ONE

Mothering Sunday Approaches

After the upheavals of the previous year, normality of a sort had returned to the north London flat shared by the young Kirrins. Workplaces were attended, gyms visited, Sundays dissatisfyingly frittered through a mild haze of hangover. Vague plans were taken up – to engage in long-term fiscal planning, to be more healthy and to take up internet dating once and for all – only to be quickly cast aside again. Which is to say that life, in general, resumed its former monotonous trot.

There was only one landmark on the horizon that threatened the new peace. It was a matter which had to be broached sooner or later, and which would require some delicacy. It was the ordinarily innocuous feast of Mother's Day which was presenting George with problems.

For there was no way, under any circumstances, that Mother's Day was to be missed this year. It must not be allowed to happen, and therefore George had taken precautions to make sure. She had fixed a calendar on the wall and circled the date; she had set various reminders on her phone and, for the preceding few weeks, had been looking up gifts.

The problem was that George had succeeded in forgetting to buy her mother a present on several other recent occasions. The first was last year's Mothering Sunday, which she had clean forgotten, plain and simple.

She had then neglected to buy her mum a birthday present, a Christmas present and also to make any acknowledgement of her parents' wedding anniversary. On each occasion, she had naturally felt worse and worse, and cursed herself ever more violently. But it didn't make any difference how much you apologized afterwards. The fact remained that you had forgotten on the day.

This Mothering Sunday, then, had taken on an almost totemic importance. George was starting to fear that, if she failed to observe one more occasion, her relationship with her mum would be permanently tarnished – altered in some subtle way that it might never be possible to repair.

George had been thinking about what best to buy her

The problem was that George had succeeded in forgetting to buy her mother a present on several other recent occasions.

mum, while taking Timmy for a walk around the park, calling out suggestions to him as she threw sticks. Timmy didn't quite hare off after sticks these days; instead, he rambled at his own gentle speed, rather like the deliberate slowness that old people employ to show their indifference to the passage of time. And so his walks were now executed at an entirely pleasant pace.

'How about a walking holiday, with Dad,' George mused, 'in the north or something?'

'Woof,' said Timmy indifferently, putting the stick back down on the ground in front of her.

She threw it again and he trundled away after it. 'Or a really nice piece of jewellery. A necklace – or a brooch,' she said.

'Woof,' said Timmy, returning with the stick thirty seconds later, still far from impressed.

'Hmm, maybe you're right,' George said. 'After all, I don't really share her taste. And it would be a lot of money to spend on something she might never use.' She threw the stick again.

'The problem is, there's one thing which I know she'd love. But it probably involves her coming to stay . . .'

Timmy dropped the stick and growled at her. This was an extremely rare occurrence and George did not like the sensation one bit.

'Don't worry, don't worry,' she reassured him. 'It won't happen. I promise. That's absolutely not on the table ...'

George's relationship with Aunt Fanny (who was so universally referred to by this name that George occasionally used it herself – and, in fact, Fanny sometimes signed notes to her daughter 'AF') had never been an entirely easy one. This, really, was down to George. Aunt Fanny could get on with practically everyone, and indeed she did. Ever since her early childhood, however, George had been what might diplomatically be called 'feisty' – although 'spiky' would be more accurate. She had a sharp and unassuageable sense of justice, which was more important to her than anything; Fanny, meanwhile, simply adored getting on with people and yearned for the quiet life.

These twin belief systems, each of which seems perfectly reasonable from the outside, brought them into unfortunate and continuous conflict. To put it simply, they just did not understand one another. To Fanny, George's

5

It was one of those relationships which is enormously improved by a buffer of about two-hundred-miles' distance.

tempers and passions were entirely incxplicable, and only ever seemed to make her unhappy. To George, Fanny was docile to an almost criminal degree.

It was one of those relationships, therefore, which is enormously improved by a buffer of about two-hundred-miles' distance. One knew that one loved the other person, and loved them dearly, so long as this abstract emotion wasn't tested by physical proximity.

What George was finding hard to ignore, though, was the obvious truth that the best Mother's Day present was a ticket to the William Morris Exhibition at the V&A. There was something about middle-aged, middle-class women that made anything with the name 'William Morris' on it entirely irresistible. It was like they had been hypnotized. Once he had been mentioned, they could, in George's experience, talk about him almost endlessly, without once managing to articulate (to someone not suffering under the delusion) what it was about him exactly that one was supposed to give a monkey's about.

And now there was a big, handsome, new exhibition of his works which was being talked about as the unmissable hot ticket of the season. Fanny would love it. And George's desire was that she receive the best Mother's Day present possible.

But the problem came when one thought about what would happen next. First, Fanny would come to stay for a few days, because the thought of spending money on a hotel when she might stay with her daughter was understandably abhorrent to her.

And shortly after she had arrived (possibly within minutes rather than hours), they would spectacularly fall out. It was not a matter of likelihood, but certainty. It was an entirely different proposition from George going to visit her parents in Dorset. There, it was understood by both parties that she was on their turf; a certain amount of pampering would be received by one party and, in the opposite direction, a certain amount of patronizing and ill-conceived advice would be tolerated and not over-reacted to.

At George's place, though, the boot was on the other foot. She prized her independence highly, and lived her life precisely as she wanted to. Yet it is the office of the mother to give advice, whether solicited or not. And, blithely heedless to the many warning signs, Aunt Fanny would undoubtedly deliver considerably more advice than George could endure. (An amount, in fact, which would earn anyone other than her mother a solid sock to the jaw.) Soon after that, the fighting would begin.

George could recall that specifically loathsome feeling she always got at the end of those rows: the ache of her shoulders as the righteous, Hulk-like rage subsided; the clarity of vision as the red mist of fury dissolved; each of them making room for the incoming tide of self-recrimination.

It didn't bear thinking about.

George threw the stick again, harder this time, as though it might hit William Morris in his beautifully decorated backside. And while Timmy wandered happily away to fetch it, she continued chewing the issue over in her mind . . .

CHAPTER TWO

Five Mess Up a Perfectly Easy Task

At this point, the reader might be wondering how it was that so nice and sensible a young person as George could have failed to purchase gifts for her mother on so many occasions. On the face of it (and this is what George feared Aunt Fanny must believe herself), it would seem thoughtless to the extent of being intentionally pointed, even callous. But the truth was more complicated and more frustrating. It went back to six months ago.

It was Dick and Anne's idea at first.

'She's such a dear,' said Anne. 'We really must do something special for her.'

'Who?' George asked, dumbfounded. 'My mum?'

'Yes!' Anne insisted. 'It suddenly struck me the other day that Aunt Fanny's like a second mum to us, and we've never really acknowledged that. All those summers, down there in Kirrin, when she used to look after us . . .'

George was still far from convinced. 'But she left us alone the whole time, and just let us bugger off all over the place – getting into all sorts of trouble in the process. I don't know if you recall—'

'Oh, *George*,' said Anne. 'They were such happy times. I wonder sometimes if I don't have a stronger relationship with your mother than I do with my own.'

If George had been feeling mean-spirited, she might have thought to herself, Well, you would, wouldn't you? You're both equally drippy. But she was not. In fact, she was rather touched by this unprompted display of filial affection.

'Well, if you want to romanticize it,' she said, 'be my guest. My memory is that we were nearly killed about two dozen times. I think Mummy should count herself lucky to have escaped a custodial sentence for neglect. But, of course, if you want to get her a present, then please do. She'll be thrilled.'

A plan was therefore arrived at to find Aunt Fanny 'the best bloody birthday present on the planet' (Dick), or 'something absolutely delightfully perfect' (Anne). Something that would (as Julian commented, when he was

11

brought in on the plot and agreed to it heartily) really 'blow her brains out', and leave her under no misapprehension about how much all the Kirrin youngsters loved her.

It was a project.

They split into teams of two and set off to different parts of town. Julian, George (and Timmy) went towards Sloane Square, to see if there was an antique or piece of jewellery that might be picked up from the shops there, while Anne and Dick went to Angel to have a look at the market in Camden Passage.

Within minutes of arriving at Angel, Dick was convinced he'd found a painting that Fanny would like. He WhatsApped a picture of it to George, who found it disturbing and inappropriate in equal measure. She phoned him.

'Is that a bull having sex?' she asked.

'Yes, I suppose it is,' said Dick, looking closer. 'But it's in the background. The rest of the picture is really very sensible and nice. Look on the left side – there's a nice pretty lady with a fan. So I thought: Fanny.'

'I can't see the photo right now because it's on my phone and I'm talking to you on my phone,' George said,

*What George was finding hard to ignore, though, was the
obvious truth that the best Mother's Day present was a
ticket to the William Morris Exhibition at the V&A.*

'but, from memory, that is not a lady with a fan – it's a clown with a machete.'

'Oh,' said Dick. 'Is it?'

'Could you put Anne on, please?'

When Anne was on the line, George wasted no time in making the situation clear to her. 'I am very fond of your brother,' she began, 'but if you allow him to take any further part in the decision-making process then it will result in physical violence.'

'Message received,' said Anne cheerfully, smiling at Dick.

'Can't you give him a wordsearch to do, or something?' George asked. 'Just park him in a pub.'

'No sooner said than done. Oh, hey, how about a darling set of little sherry glasses? I can see them in this shop window.'

'Hmm,' said George. 'Good idea on paper, but actually she hardly drinks, and they have very few visitors to entertain. Keep looking, though.'

'Will do! Loveyoubye.'

Dick was mightily relieved to be deposited in a nearby coffee house, where he was instructed to attempt the quick crossword and see how many Frappuccino flavours hc could try in an hour.

'I'll start with hazelnut toffee supreme. Or maybe salted marshmallow . . .' he said, his eyes roaming over the board.

'Fine, sounds great,' said Anne over her shoulder, through the closing door. Within ten minutes of solo present-hunting, she had found what she thought was a pretty spot-on gift. She phoned George again.

'What?' said George testily.

'How about an original Wedgwood teapot?'

She heard George catch her breath. 'How much?'

Anne cleared her throat. 'Not cheap,' she said. 'But it's from all of us. And it's a very special present. It's a birthday-Christmas-birthday and so on present. Mostly from George, of course – but also from Dick, Julian and myself, I mean.'

'Send me a pic,' said George. 'I think that sounds amazing. Because, you'll never guess what: we've found the same thing.'

'No way!' said Anne.

'Ten quid says ours is better!' Julian yelled in the background.

There was the muffled thunder of a hand covering the microphone, but Anne could still hear George's voice. 'Julian, shut up; you'll get us chucked out of here ...' Then there was a pause, and Anne heard George add, 'Look, Julian, here's a tenner; why don't you go to that pub on the corner ...'

But Julian was not to be so easily dissuaded from his duty. Today was the last shopping-and-shipping day before Aunt Fanny's birthday and so the deal had to be concluded within business hours. Julian (emboldened by a pint or two of Moretti over lunch) felt he was the man to make it happen.

The first hiccup came when the antiques seller announced his preferred price. Julian coughed wheezingly to hide his shock and struggled to regain his composure as he dragged George to the other end of the shop.

'He's trying to fleece us,' he said with conviction. 'It's barely worth half that. Tell you what, let's go to the pub on the corner and I'll look up what these things normally go for online ...'

They retreated, under the glassily ambivalent stare of the antiques dealer, to the pub three doors along, where

Julian rinsed the battery on his smartphone looking up similar items on eBay.

'Stupid pissing phone with its useless damned reception,' he muttered bitterly, before looking up, realizing how loudly he had been talking and offering an insipid smile to the two elderly gentlemen at the next table. 'I thought we were in London,' he muttered, fiddling with the controls as George returned from the bar with a brandy and soda for him and a ginger beer for herself. '4G my hairy backside . . .' he said. 'Oh, thanks. Hey, I think that price might not be all that terrible after all. But let's offer him two hundred smackers less than it's worth, and see if he meets us halfway . . .'

They were back in the antiques dealership within two swift swigs of the tumbler, and affecting penury.

'Could we perhaps . . . I mean, we *love* the item . . .' began Julian beseechingly.

'Too bloody expensive,' said George. 'Knock off two hundred quid and perhaps we can talk.'

The antiques dealer made them a gift of his quiet, silky laugh. 'That's not going to happen,' he said.

Negotiations then began in earnest, which also involved

'Yes!' Anne insisted. 'It suddenly struck me the other day
that Aunt Fanny's like a second mum to us, and we've
never really acknowledged that.'

a sequence of phone calls to Anne. In Islington, the teapot was taken out of its cabinet and held up to be photographed. Both sellers were clearly interested in the business, and content to be toyed with in this way for the time being. It was, at long last (with the winter afternoon drawing in), estimated that the Angel item was of marginally better quality, as well as being slightly cheaper.

Anne hung up the phone and turned back to the proprietor to tell him he had a sale on his hands – which, from the overheard murmurings of her conversation, he had already intuited – and perhaps it was because she was so beautiful and had been so charming to deal with that he was holding the teapot so lightly. For, at that moment, Dick (who was surfing on twin giddy highs of sugar and caffeine) entered the shop as quietly as he could behind them and, as he closed the door, let out a burp of which no one, to look at him, would have supposed him capable.

The sherry glasses in the window vibrated, not just to the sound that Dick had emitted, but also (immediately afterwards) to the consequent sound of a very valuable piece of china shattering on the floor.

There followed a flurry of apologies from Anne and

stern-lipped responses from the shop owner. And soon thereafter another flurry, this time of phone calls to George and Julian, to try to alert them to return to the shop and buy the teapot they had had their eye on. But it seemed that in the intervening few minutes George and Julian had passed back within one of London's mysterious coverage blind spots, and neither of their phones had reception.

(They would not afterwards admit this, but they were in fact having a pint of cider in the downstairs room at the pub on the corner, doing the Saturday *Guardian* quiz and arguing about the titles of Elvis Costello albums.)

So it was that the four (five, if you included Timmy) had failed to buy a suitable gift in time for Aunt Fanny's birthday. They smarted beneath this failure, especially considering their intentions had been so pure. And they determined that, for Christmas, Aunt Fanny would have the best damned present a favoured aunt (and mother) had ever received.

CHAPTER THREE

Five Bugger Something Up Again, Despite It Appearing Objectively Quite Achievable

'So, Christmas,' said Julian. 'This time, we're going to get Aunt Fanny's gift just right. Just right.'

'Okay, fine,' said George. 'But this time I have a veto on it; is that fair?'

'Of course you do,' said Anne. 'Of course. We don't want a repeat of that horror.' The insulting words of the shop owner were still ringing in her ears. 'Anything you think,' she added.

'I was thinking that there's a space in the hall, when you come in the house, in Kirrin,' said George, 'where the floor's rather bare. And that might be filled with a nice rug.'

'Smashing idea,' said Julian, who was lolling on the sofa. 'I know a really good place in Mayfair . . .'

George chewed her lip. She had heard Julian say

things like this before. Unfortunately, his taste was wildly scatter-gun. Occasionally it was perfect – that could not be denied. But, more often than not, not.

'I'll come with you,' she said.

'So will I,' said Dick.

Everything went brilliantly. Everything, that is, except Aunt Fanny actually receiving the gift. They attended the shop and found that, despite being expensive, there was a rug which was not only beautiful, but borderline affordable as well. They bought it in full knowledge that it would enhance the hall of Fanny and Quentin's Dorset house no small amount, and left the shop with a deeply satisfying sensation of pride.

It was as Dick crossed the road with the carpet under one arm that he caught sight of a snug little pub on the corner of the street. It was pushing two thirty, and none of them had eaten lunch, so they needed very little persuasion to alter course in that direction, barge in and grab a table in the corner.

They had a few pints. Dick had the scampi and chips, which the pub had the audacity to list as a 'special'; Julian had a disappointing salad and stole most of Dick's chips;

Everything went brilliantly. Everything, that is, except Aunt Fanny actually receiving the gift.

and George had a chicken burger. As the afternoon wore on, they exchanged a sequence of increasingly insalubrious anecdotes and eventually tumbled out of the pub about dinner time to make their way to Bond Street Tube station.

It was Julian who suggested they have just one more pint when they got off the Tube at the other end. The mood of the group was decidedly jolly – that is, until they got home after four further pints and realized they could not remember the last time they'd been in possession of Aunt Fanny's present.

George had the pleasure, the next day, of waking to the combination of a hangover and the knowledge that she had to come up with a Christmas gift for her mum over the course of a morning – her train home was already booked for lunchtime. Rather than be proactive about it, however, she spent a bad-tempered hour on the phone to the London Underground lost-property department, and, in so doing, wasted her one chance of getting her mother a good present.

When they met (Aunt Fanny had been in town to go Christmas shopping, and they were catching the same train home), she accepted the story about the lost gift with a somewhat muted expression. She was, for once, very hard to read. It wasn't that she disbelieved her daughter, exactly. But the fumes of alcohol coming from the opposite seat in the railway carriage were unmistakable. And this failure to buy presents was turning into a habit with George . . .

George ran through the events again in her head as she walked home, see-sawing between feelings of guilt and self-justification. She ignored a call from Julian, and then one from Anne. She was feeling ruminative and not in the mood to chat.

No, whatever her present to Aunt Fanny was to be this Mother's Day, it was certainly not going to involve her cousins. She wasn't going to give them a chance to muck things up a third time.

'After you,' she said, holding the apartment's front door for Timmy.

'Woof,' he said gratefully, slipping inside.

George took the stairs slowly, trying to think what the right present would be – what it *could* be – to sufficiently impress and distract her mother, and prevent her from coming to town.

The alternative, of course, was for George to get her to come to town and stay in the flat, while George absented herself. That would take some thinking and planning, though.

As she reached the first floor, her phone rang. It was Dick.

'Really,' she said. 'What is it that can't wait ten seconds? I'm just outside . . .' Her key was already in the lock, but Dick's sombre voice arrested her hand in mid turn.

'I just wanted to warn you,' he said. 'To give you a bit of a heads-up.'

'Why? About what? Why are you speaking so quietly?'

'I'm in the bathroom. Trying not to be overheard . . .'

'Overheard by who?' she asked. It sounded like Dick was playing some sort of game or prank. George was not in the mood. She rang off, then opened the door and went in.

'Hello, darling,' said Aunt Fanny.

CHAPTER FOUR

Worst-case Scenario

George goggled at her. Each new detail she saw appalled her more. Aunt Fanny had brought not one but two suit-cases, and she was smiling like someone who had just done something a little bit daring and adventurous. And George could tell from the attitudes of her housemates that Fanny had already revealed her intentions, and that it was not good news.

Anne and Julian were sitting on the settee, wearing expressions of painful politeness. Dick was returning from the bathroom, putting his phone in his pocket and looking haunted.

Timmy was in his basket, his paws over his eyes.

'I thought I'd come and stay for a few days!' Aunt Fanny said, and now George knew the worst.

George was an expert excuse comer-up-wither. When on form, she could hardly be bettered. But to come up with

27

'I must say, I like the relaxed atmosphere you have here –
how you don't worry too much about tidying up. I wish I
could be the same . . .'

a really convincing reason why Aunt Fanny couldn't stay, off the top of her head, when Aunt Fanny was already *in the process* of staying, was beyond the powers of even the most formidable improviser.

George swallowed.

'Great,' she said. 'Great.' She nodded a dozen times and then looked over at her housemates. They reflected her empty smile back at her.

'Great,' said George a third time, and nodded again.

'Well, come over and give me a kiss then,' said her mother. 'I'm sorry to surprise you like this; it was just a mad impulse. It was your father who suggested it, in fact. He's been working on one of his experiments around the clock and getting all . . . well, you know how he gets . . .'

They've had a row, George thought. And he's chucked her out. Perhaps she tried to tidy his office again.

'. . . And rather than getting under his feet, I decided to go away. Then I read in the Sunday papers about this new William Morris exhibition . . .'

Bugger it, George thought.

At first glance, and to uneducated eyes, it might seem a trifle presumptuous for a parent to pitch up unannounced at the home of their offspring in this way. But Fanny's behaviour can be explained by the fact that the flat in which her daughter, niece and nephews lived had been paid for by Uncle Quentin. On paper (a purely theoretical piece of paper – there was no tenancy agreement), it was the youngsters, therefore, who were inconveniencing her, with their somewhat stop-start payments of decidedly below-market-value rent.

Naturally, she usually gave far more notice than this before a visit. But the understanding was that, when any Kirrin parent came to stay, Dick would sleep on the spare mattress beneath Anne's bed and vacate his own room. It was perhaps this that accounted for how haunted he now looked, as he had only in the last sixty seconds completed an urgent and frantic cleaning of his room.

Seeing how horrified her cousins were, George realized that she must put a brave face on it and make conversation. So she filled the kettle, fetched some biscuits and asked her mother how the journey had been.

Slowly, the others made their way forward from the sofa to the kitchen area. They asked tentatively if Fanny had many things planned for the next few days.

'No, not a thing – aside from the exhibition. Do you have any particular recommendations?'

Like most Londoners, the flatmates paid absolutely no attention to the things that visitors to the city found interesting. It would feel entirely odd, to them, to make a trip to the Shard, say, just for the reason of visiting. Some secondary purpose, like a friend's birthday, would be necessary to get them there. The only events which caught their attention in the capital were new pop-up restaurants, murders and the occasional film premiere, which they read about the next day over the shoulders of fellow commuters. They all collectively shrugged.

'Oh, you lot are useless,' said Fanny. 'I'll have to read up myself about what's on offer. I'd love to take you out for dinner, of course, as it's so nice to see you . . . and maybe the theatre would be nice . . .'

For Aunt Fanny, a trip to London wasn't complete without a visit to the National Theatre, a few hours at John Lewis, a look round Liberty for fabric, and lunch at one of the more affordable imitators of Fortnum and Mason.

The younger Kirrin generation, however, considered that a visit to London wasn't really authentic without packing oneself among the other miserable sardines on the Northern Line in rush hour, donating various sums of money to half a dozen suspiciously well-dressed, but scrupulously polite beggars, staring at several miles of grimy pavement while walking through the whipping cold, and spending an evening drinking at an ear-splittingly rammed craft-beer pub, before having a kebab on the way home. But this was not a vision of life that they felt like foisting on their older relative.

So what diversions should they recommend to Aunt Fanny, then?

Fanny's mention of a trip to the theatre made George feel lethargic and morose. George loathed the theatre because actors were, without exception, a bunch of stupid, preening berks. Somehow, in movies, one didn't notice so much – the film-makers were able to cut around it, and one got distracted by the location photography, the costumes, the action and so on. (George's film star of choice was Jeremy Statham.) On the stage, one was unable to escape the dreadful posturing stupidity of it all. She rubbed her eyes to hide a grimace.

The prospect of eating out with Fanny – as all four Kirrin

*The prospect of eating out with Fanny – as all
four Kirrin children knew only too well –
was an even ghastlier one.*

children knew only too well – was an even ghastlier one. She could be an exquisitely kind and thoughtful person, and she was the perfect host to a T. But being served in a restaurant brought about a kind of werewolf-like transformation in her and she became appallingly offensive to bar staff and waiters.

It had, in fact, been the subject of one of the four's grimmer pub chats – the speculation that Aunt Fanny's unthinking rudeness had been responsible for them consuming any amount of cooks' spit, bogeys and worse. It was not a position they had any intention of putting themselves in again.

Instead, they all started making noises about having all sorts of leftovers to eat, or being on a diet, and quickly persuaded Fanny that it would be much nicer and more intimate for them all to make her dinner each night and eat at home.

'*Lovely*,' said Aunt Fanny. 'What a treat. And maybe one night I can cook for you too. I must say, I like the relaxed atmosphere you have here – how you don't worry too much about tidying up. I wish I could be the same . . .'

Dick went to make final adjustments to his room; Anne

did the same to hers, pulling out the spare bed and hunting for the joss sticks, which would be necessary each morning to neutralize Dick's nightly expressions.

The others were somewhat guiltily dreading a lengthy evening of family discussions. But in the event, once the rooms were ready, Aunt Fanny proclaimed herself exhausted and begged to be allowed to retire.

CHAPTER FIVE

So It Begins

George had an unhappy night of disturbing dreams in which she was the child of a giant marauding cockroach, which she first ran from, and then finally destroyed with a piercing blow from an oversized safety pin. On waking, in the morning, she remembered her dream and felt (of course) guilty about it. Being a daughter seemed to involve feeling guilty about something or other, most of the time.

It won't be that bad, she thought. Just push on through. You're in your twenties now; you're not a teenager. You don't need to let her press your buttons. Show her you're a grown-up and she'll respect that.

Coming into the kitchen, George found her mother already up (it was seven a.m.) and busying herself at the cooker.

'Nice to see you up and about,' Fanny said pleasantly, 'and not wasting the best part of the day.'

'I'm not twelve *anymore, for Christ's sake,'* was the barked
retort which rose to her lips.

'Yeah, well, it's part of having a job, I suppose,' said George. 'Wasting the best part of the day is rather frowned upon in office work. What's that you're cooking?'

'Your favourite,' her mother said. 'Porridge with currants and honey. And a little salt.'

Here, then, was George's first test. Already, with this initial gesture, her daily routine was being tampered with – something which, in the ordinary course of events, she found utterly intolerable. And now she would be expected to respond to it sweetly.

'I'm not *twelve* anymore, for Christ's sake,' was the barked retort which rose to her lips. She ground her teeth to keep from saying it.

'Thanks,' she said. 'Do you want a cup of tea?'

'I've made some, but it will be getting stewy by now. You didn't have any English breakfast, so I used the last of the Earl Grey.'

George had a strict rule that any tea more complicated than straightforward builder's (with no sugar) was an exercise in pretension and facile time-wasting. So she poured herself a cooling mug of liquid that managed somehow to be both oily and pallid, then sipped it with pursed lips.

'I don't usually eat porridge anymore,' she said, taking a mouthful. 'Er, I haven't, really, since I was about twelve.'

'Oh,' said her mum. 'But you used to *love* it.'

'Well, I used to eat it,' said George fairly. 'But I wasn't particularly fond of it, actually.'

'Oh,' said Fanny again. 'Well. I'm sorry.'

'This is delicious, though!' George said, just too late to prevent a visible twitch crossing her mother's face, indicative of repressed sadness. George's head swam. Usually she didn't have to speak to anyone at all until about ten in the morning, by which time she was tucking into her third coffee of the day. This emotional slalom was quite beyond her. She closed her eyes.

'I'll leave you to get ready for work.'

'Mummy, please—'

'I can see you're in one of your moods,' Fanny said, as she pootled off to her room.

CHAPTER SIX

A Nice Evening In

George's colleagues were used to the fact that she could be 'spirited' – although 'confrontational' would have been more just. But none of them knew that they had, until now, been drifting through life in a state of serene innocence with regard to how bad George *could* be, when provoked.

And she was, of course, on this particular Tuesday morning, deeply provoked.

It had always been a special ability of Aunt Fanny's to get under George's skin by the casual deployment of a seemingly innocent phrase. And, although she would hotly deny it, she knew perfectly well that 'I can see you're in one of your moods' was the most potent weapon in her arsenal. It provoked a stream of conflicting negative emotions which, once started, could flow, self-replenishing, for hours.

The mixture included self-recrimination, powerlessness,

rage, hurt and a smorgasbord of other feelings that could not be listed comprehensively in fewer than half a dozen pages. George bubbled with fury throughout her commute to work and discovered she had listened to an entire episode of 'The Feminist Cricketer' podcast without hearing a word.

By eleven, her colleagues had all spotted or alerted each other to the fact that she was to be left alone (for at least a day) and, after spending a few hours in comparative peace – albeit one which swirled with self-doubt and an alarming feeling that she was about to cry – George WhatsApped her cousins.

They had set up a group a few months ago so that they could alert each other during the day to various house issues, such as what kitchen items were needed, who was around for dinner and so on. The messages mostly consisted of Dick making facile jokes and Anne asking him please to be serious for once. Julian usually ignored the messages as an impertinent intrusion into his working day and the battery life of his phone, while George's contributions were usually terse, at best.

When they received George's message that lunchtime, though, they all immediately knew that now was the time to rally round, as one of their number was in trouble. It was the tone of the message that first struck them: it just sounded so unGeorgelike.

> PLEEZ help me to look after my mum; next
> few days will be really difficult, i can tell already;
> i ReALLY dont want to fall out w her; please, i don't
> ask you fr mch ☺ ☺

The smiley emojis really sealed the deal.

'Bloody hell,' muttered Julian, as he read it. He was deeply alarmed – enough even to overlook his dislike for the use of semicolons without a preceding colon. 'This calls for action.'

George was astounded by how moved she was by the messages which came quickly back, from each of her cousins. *We won't let you down*, they assured her. *We're going to be the best damned surrogate children Aunt Fanny has ever had*, Dick said. *We'll charm her bollocks off*, said Julian. *Of course, my darling angel*, said

It had always been a special ability of Aunt Fanny's to get under George's skin by the casual deployment of a seemingly innocent phrase.

Anne, followed by: *Julian, why must you be so utterly foul?*

Thus, as was so common among the group of friends, they decided to work together. And, before they knew it, a plan was arrived at.

That evening, they planned to arrive home within a few minutes of each other. They had brainstormed an evening of things that Aunt Fanny would like, and which would pleasantly distract her.

There was a new series of Scandi noir (concerning a sequence of inventively gruesome murders in a Swedish clown college) they had just missed on BBC4, which Dick had promised to procure on DVD.

Aunt Fanny loved baking and cakes, so Anne said she would buy the ingredients for her personal culinary masterpiece: a chocolate sponge cake with a fresh raspberry and crème fraîche filling.

Julian's allotted task was to make his famous flambéed duck breast with honey-glazed carrots and potato dauphinois.

George's only job was simply to return home, albeit

burdened with guilt and a sense of impending failure. But knowing that she dreaded it, the others spent the afternoon sending her messages of reassurance that all would be well.

She was first back to a house that looked subtly, but disturbingly, different. She couldn't put her finger on what it was, but something had changed. She nosed around for a few moments, like a character in a science-fiction film who has just awoken and can't yet be sure whether they are in the real world or a dream.

'I bought you a present,' said her mother, from behind her. George jumped.

'I hope you don't mind,' said Fanny, 'but I thought the flat needed it.' She stood aside to reveal a new Hoover.

'Oh,' said George. 'Well, that *is* nice.'

'I know you had one already, but it was really on its last legs,' Fanny said. 'It was our old one from Kirrin Cottage, which I bought to help with your asthma.'

'Of course,' said George. 'Yes. It is rather old, I suppose. Thank you, Mummy.'

'I had to bring it back on the bus from John Lewis. Took an absolute age! I nearly finished the new William

Thus, as was so common among the group of friends,
they decided to work together. And, before they knew it,
a plan was arrived at.

Boyd audiobook. It's *good*,' she said, in a voice that sounded rather unsure, 'but not as good as *Restless*. I loved that one.'

'I know you did,' said George.

'I just thought it was refreshing that it was a *man* writing about a *woman*, in a man's world.'

'I remember you saying.'

'The ladies in the book group loved that one too. Oh, hello Dick, hello Anne. Don't mind me,' she screamed above the noise of the new Hoover, which, during the preceding exchange, she had plugged in. 'I just thought I'd do a BIT OF CLEANING. I feel like the flat PERHAPS NEEDS IT.'

Dick and Anne had both been planning to make a big entrance and talk the hind legs off their aunt to divert her attention from her daughter. But this was rendered impossible by the loud shrieking of the Hoover, and the sight of an upper-middle-class woman of a certain age bent over it, whumpfing it forward and back over the carpet like her life depended on it.

Dick sat on the sofa next to George (who lay down and put her feet on his lap), while Anne wordlessly went to the open kitchen area and began her baking preparations. Dick and George (and, shortly, Julian) watched the determined relentlessness of Aunt Fanny's cleaning with irritation at first, but they soon started to find it funny. That wore off quite quickly, though, and they went back to being irritated again. George habitually took about seven minutes to do the hoovering when it was her turn to clean the flat. Dick had once secretly managed to do it in three, an achievement of which he felt equally proud and ashamed.

Aunt Fanny was really going to town on it, though, and hit the half-hour mark without breaking stride. She was pulling back pieces of furniture and really giving the nooks and crannies a good seeing to. It started to feel rather as though she was making a point. At last, the Hoover emitted a descending wheeze, and Aunt Fanny straightened, putting a hand to her back.

'Thank Christ for that,' whispered Julian. 'At least now I can hear myself thi—'

But at this moment, Anne turned on her Kenwood mixer in the kitchen, only ten feet away, which gave out a sound just a semitone higher than that of the Hoover. Dick and George watched as Julian delivered a volley of exasperated swearing that was thankfully inaudible to them.

Julian got up to go to his room, possibly so that he could continue swearing in peace, and the moment he had done so, Anne switched off the mixer. Then she opened a cupboard, looking for the caster sugar, and let out an exclamation of surprise.

'What's this?' she asked in puzzlement.

'Oh,' said Fanny, coming into the kitchen area. 'I just popped to the shops to buy a few things; I hope you don't mind . . .'

'Not at all,' said Anne, taking down a tin of beans from her baking cupboard.

'I might not have put everything in the right place,' said Fanny. 'I had to guess.'

'No, that's fine,' said Anne, opening the dried goods cupboard to find it stocked with dog food. 'So, where's the sugar?'

'Down there,' said Fanny, pointing to a lower cupboard. Anne opened it and retrieved the sugar from between the bleach and the rat poison. She then spent a fruitless few minutes looking in the fridge for the butter. She could feel her temperature rising. If she didn't get this cake on soon, she'd have to share the kitchen with Julian, with his high-handed comments and his messy ways, which she had no intention of doing, if she could avoid it . . .

'*Where* is the butter?' she asked at last, waving her hands at the empty fridge. 'How have you made it disappear?'

'Butter doesn't need to be in the fridge,' said Aunt Fanny. 'And besides, I thought it was a shame not to use that lovely little butter dish. It was a wedding present to us from Granny B.'

Anne nodded curtly and snatched the butter dish up. There was nothing more frustrating, she thought to herself, as she sought out the electronic scales and cocoa powder, than helplessly rooting around from cupboard to cupboard in a strange kitchen. It made one feel so clumsy and stupid. And there was something even more annoying when that strange kitchen was your own . . .

Anne did at length get the cake in the oven just in time to vacate the kitchen before Julian got going with dinner. While George played with Timmy a few feet away in the living room, Dick opened the bottle of Prosecco he'd brought home. Aunt Fanny gave a seagull cry of delight on being offered a glass, and an endearing guffaw when it was pointed out she was still wearing the pinny she'd put on for cleaning.

'I wore one of these to a restaurant once. I was halfway through my main course before I noticed. When I asked Quentin why he hadn't told me, he said he thought it was part of the costume. The brute.'

'Ha!' said Julian. 'Typical man.'

'Typical Daddy,' said George, happy that the mood in the flat was starting to warm up a bit.

'Sit down, why don't you; the food won't be long at all,' said Julian. 'Ah, bonza! Thanks, Dick.' And he downed his glass of Prosecco in one.

Sitting on the living-room floor, George rubbed Timmy behind the ears. She was reassured to be here with her friends. She wondered whether, against all the odds, perhaps things might after all be okay, and she might get through this dinner – and perhaps this whole visit – without falling out with her mother.

She was, for once, being mistakenly optimistic.

CHAPTER SEVEN

Dinner Date

Although he hardly ever bothered, when he turned his hand to it, Julian was a masterful chef. As long as he was frequently lubricated with whatever wine was to hand, he was, as a cook, precise, swift and confident, and consistently produced dishes which drew gratifying gasps of pleasure. So it was today.

'There was this business with Mrs Coffrey – do you know her?' Aunt Fanny was saying, as they all neared the end of their main course.

'No, I don't,' said George.

'You were at school with her son, Simon. Simon Coffrey?'

George shrugged.

'Well, anyway, her husband died last year, which was very sad, and she's been ever so depressed. And she's just been pushing people away. It's so sad.'

George noted her own temper straining, threatening to shift up a gear. Anne and Dick, too, felt the atmosphere change for the worse.

'But, Mummy,' George said, 'I don't know who this person is.'

'And her sister, Carol, is in a bad way too. She's been suffering from this mystery bleeding . . .'

Julian allowed his fork to clatter noisily on to his plate. Aunt Fanny looked up.

'More wine?' he asked.

'Oh, no, not for me, thank you,' said Fanny. 'I hardly drink anything these days. Of course, they think it's cancer.'

'What is?' Anne asked, alarmed.

'The bleeding. But it's what *type* of cancer, of course.'

'I think I'll have another glass,' said Julian, getting up. 'I seem to have lost my appetite.'

'Don't pick your nose, darling,' said Fanny. 'It's so unappealing.'

'Well, I'm not trying to get off with you, am I?'

'I just want you to meet someone nice, and you won't if you go around doing that all the time. And I wish you'd go to the dentist – it'll save you money in the long run, you know.'

George noted her temper straining, threatening to shift

54

up a gear. Anne and Dick, too, felt the atmosphere change for the worse. George felt her temper bucking and rearing like a beast, threatening to overrule her reason. But she had been fearing this moment all day, and was monitoring her feelings as closely and dispassionately as she could. By forcing her breathing to slow and reminding herself a) how important this was, b) how soon it would be over and c) how unpleasant it would be for the others if she made a scene, George at last, and by the narrowest margin, succeeded in reining her temper in.

She counted to five.

Then she turned to her mother and nodded. And smiled.

Anne and Dick relaxed. They felt like innocent bystanders in a Western saloon, after a narrowly avoided shoot-out. Julian was glugging wine and didn't notice.

'What are you up to tomorrow, Fanny?' Anne asked brightly.

'Ah, well, my ticket for the exhibition is at eleven. And then I wondered whether we might meet up for lunch?'

There was a small pause as the youngsters all made rapid geographical calculations. Because they lived together, it'd never occurred to them to meet for lunch before. But, now they thought about it, it was perfectly feasible. And, of course, it didn't occur to Dick, Anne or Julian to make excuses – rallying round was the order of the day.

'Soho is roughly in the middle of where we all work,' said Dick. 'Somewhere Chinese, maybe?'

Aunt Fanny shook her head. 'Oh, no, that really disagrees with me. I just can't stomach it. Why don't I try to book Fortnum's, as it's a special occasion?'

'Fortnum's,' declared Julian, now comfortably into his fifth glass of wine, 'is a tourist trap. I know where we should go. The Montagu Pyke!'

Aunt Fanny was impressed, both by this rather exciting and austere-sounding name, and by the confidence with which Julian asserted it. Clearly, he knew his onions. She said she was looking forward to it.

Aunt Fanny then insisted on doing the washing-up, which Anne (the dryer-upper) watched out of the corner of her eye with disapproval, spotting the many grease marks which escaped her aunt's vigilance, but not feeling it was sporting to point them out.

DINNER DATE

By now, Julian had rolled to bed rather the worse for wear, and the others soon followed suit. Timmy, who spent most of the time in his bed, anyway, had been asleep for the past hour.

CHAPTER EIGHT

Lunch in England's Canteen

The next morning, at work, the four housemates all tried to put to the forefront of their minds what they liked about Aunt Fanny. When they went to visit her in Kirrin, she always seemed so ecstatic to see them and took such evident pleasure in making them feel relaxed and welcome.

They suspected that the reason it was so different this time was something subtly psychological to do with territory. With her in their house, each party was in a different position, meaning the power dynamic between them had been tinkered with in some crucial way, taking almost all the joy out of the relationship.

Aunt Fanny seemed an entirely different creature in this new setting – and the difference was in no way an improvement. She asked constant questions about each young relative's relationship status, and gave presumptuous advice about their finances. In repose, there was something rigid and dogmatic in her expression – depressive, even – and when she woke up out of this state and made a pleasant face, it was with visible effort. Also, she ate in a peculiar, slightly finicky way, and often left what looked like the tastiest bits of the meal. She had turned from someone they thought they knew inside out into another, strange, less pleasant person. Perhaps this was what getting old entailed, they thought dismally.

If anything, George's cousins (who had expected to find George the difficult one to deal with over these few days) sympathized with her a great deal. Thus they made sure they arrived for lunch in good time.

Aunt Fanny toddled along at one on the dot, and found them at a table not far from the door.

'What is this place?' she asked. 'It's not quite what I was expecting . . .'

'Welcome to England's canteen,' said Julian. 'Now you can say you've had lunch in a Wetherspoon's!'

Aunt Fanny found it all rather intriguing. She was the sort of woman who felt at home in the café at Marks and Spencer's, or at the National Gallery, and so this was rather exotic to her. The other tables around them ('It's

'What was I like as a baby?' Anne asked.
'Fat,' said Aunt Fanny simply. Anne looked as though she
had been connected to the National Grid.

enormous, this place!' she said) were mostly occupied by people who were young, old or foreign. There were Russian and Polish accents aplenty, and the two old Irish men at the next table contributed to the atmosphere by shouting at each other aggressively, then laughing, then shouting aggressively again and laughing again, on what appeared to be a continuous basis.

'It's certainly very reasonable ...' Aunt Fanny said, looking at the menu. 'I think I'll just have a sandwich ...'

The others, who had been mildly apprehensive at Julian's choice for lunch venue, were pleased that she found Wetherspoon's so diverting. They insisted (pointing to the very reasonableness she had already remarked upon) that she have something hot, at the very least.

She perused the menu again and then let out an exclamation of delight. 'Steak and kidney pudding!' she said. 'I haven't had one of those for years. And spotted dick too! My favourite!'

'Easy,' said Dick.

Julian had noticed that the menu now included calorific counts next to each dish, which for him added another *frisson* to the ordering process. 'If I go for the surf and turf, with the option of onion rings, that seems to be the maximum . . .' he said. 'Ah, no. Hahah! Here it is. The Philly cheesesteak. A whopping sixteen hundred calories! Yes, please! God bless Philadelphia.'

'I'm sure it's very authentic,' said Dick. 'It's probably made in a factory in Carmarthenshire and, at this end, just bunged in an industrial microwave for forty seconds.'

'Well, that's where you're wrong, actually, Captain Snarkypants,' said Julian, who was already cheering up markedly owing to his first pint of Doom Bar. 'Everything here is artificial; it is the very artificiality of the experience that gives it its own . . . I don't know . . . *ersatz* authenticity. Or do I mean *gestalt*?'

Dick always zoned out when Julian started talking like this. And Julian didn't strictly need anyone listening to him either. As long as he could pretend to himself there was someone paying attention, he could discourse at length, like a lecturer, talking up into the air and marvelling at his own loquacity.

Instead, Dick turned to Fanny and George, and was alarmed to discover that leaving them alone for even this short time was perilous. He could tell at once that

Aunt Fanny was offering unwelcome advice – she had tilted her head back, and was literally talking down her nose. George was hunched and defensive, her expression thunderous, while Anne, between them, looked meek and helpless.

Dick decided not to wait and find out what was going on, but to blunder in and take advantage of his reputation as a poor listener.

'Aunt Fanny,' he said loudly.

'Yes,' she said, turning to him. It was true, there was more steel in those eyes now than he had ever noticed before. Something almost cold.

'Aunt Fanny,' was as far ahead as Dick had thought. He struggled. All three women looked at him. (It didn't help that, over his shoulder, he could hear Julian waffling on: '. . . which I suppose one could say has a certain antiseptic quality . . .' he was saying.)

'Do you . . .' Dick began, and looked up at the ceiling. The longer the pause, the more thoughtful it made him seem – which panicked him, as it gave the impression that he was about to say something momentous. Which he definitely wasn't.

'Like . . .' he added. He had them on tenterhooks now. 'Do you like' was definitely a way to start a sentence. But which sentence, to be exact? What could he possibly end it with? What could he, Dick, possibly be asking his aunt about? The new series of *Daredevil* on Netflix? What her Uber rating was? What?

'Are you going on holiday this summer?' Dick finished in a rush.

'"Do you like are you going on holiday this summer"?' George asked. 'Dick, what the bloody hell are you talking about?'

'I was asking your mother, actually. So,' said Dick. 'Fanny.'

'Oh, no, we never go anywhere,' said Fanny. 'Quentin always has his work. That's the trouble with being married to someone who loves what they do – going away is a chore for them. So I tend to go off by myself, and pootle around the country, visiting people.'

'Like now,' said Dick.

'Yes,' she said. 'Like now.'

She spoke placidly, with her hands in her lap like a schoolgirl. She certainly didn't look like someone who was on holiday. What *is* up with her? Dick thought. It's something. She said that at a temperature of around freezing point. I wonder what's going on?

'Darling, I really *do* wish you'd go to the dentist,' Fanny suddenly remarked to her daughter.

'I know, I know, I will,' said George.

'I just worry about your teeth,' Fanny said. 'I lie awake at night sometimes, thinking about it. How about if I pay for you to go? I'd be happy to . . .'

'It's really not necessary,' said George, digging in. 'I promise I'll go in the next few weeks. I promise.'

'It's just, if you wait, it gets so expensive, darling . . .' said Fanny.

'*I know that,*' said George, now at risk of damaging her teeth further, so hard was she gritting them.

At last, Fanny dimly seemed to perceive that she wasn't really winning her daughter over, so she turned to her nephew.

'How about you, Dick?' she asked. 'Have you got someone special in your life?'

'Well, you did ask me that twice last night and the answer's still no, I'm afraid.'

'You should go on this new computer thing, what's it called. Kindling?'

'Kindle? You think I should read more books?' Dick said. 'Probably true.'

'No, no, I mean ... What's that one called?' Fanny asked.

'Facebook?' George said.

'Oh, darling, even *I've* heard of Facebook,' Fanny said. 'I'm not impossibly ancient, you know. The one with the funny name.'

'Google,' said Julian. 'Periscope. Spotify. Deliveroo?'

'No, no,' she said.

'Chumbucket?' he suggested.

'What's that?' Fanny asked.

Julian had been expecting her to pass straight over this without blinking. At being asked to explain it, he perked up. 'Well,' he reflected, 'it's a social-media app for people to make friends in the world of, er –' he looked around the room – 'competitive saltwater angling.'

'How fascinating,' said Fanny politely.

'This conversation has really gone off the rails,' said George.

*'The problem is, it probably involves Mummy
coming to stay . . .' said George.
Timmy dropped the stick and growled at her.*

'Make friends . . .' said Fanny, trying to find the thread. Julian's phrase had stirred something in her mind. 'Oh, yes, that's it! Grinder. Dick, you should try that.'

Dick looked rather awkward. 'I'm not sure I'd really fit in that, you know, scene, to be honest.'

Light had dawned on George's face. 'She means Tinder,' she said.

'That's it!' Fanny said. 'Tinder, kindling – both to do with fire. That's why I got them mixed up.'

'Tinder. Right. Yes, well, we'll see,' said Dick. 'I don't seem to be too worried about it at the moment. Happy just bumbling along as I am.'

Aunt Fanny didn't reply to this, only regarded him quietly. 'And your job,' she said at last. 'Your mother tells me you don't really enjoy it. I'm sorry to hear that . . .'

'Oh, well,' said Dick, shrugging. 'It's not too bad, I suppose . . . But I'm not really crazy about it, if I'm honest, no.'

'So, are you applying for other places?'

Dick looked pained. He felt he was being backed into a corner. 'Not quite at the moment, er . . .' he said. 'But I will soon.' He nodded rather uncertainly, and realized that his previous sentence both sounded like, and was, an utter lie.

'How about that place you worked last summer?' Fanny asked, in a voice one would normally use to encourage a four-year-old to join in with the other children at a party. 'You loved that, didn't you?'

'Yeees, I did,' said Dick. He felt rather rattled, as though he was being examined – he had to wrack his brains even for answers he knew perfectly well. 'But I was just an intern there. They've not got a job going. I wrote to them a few months ago and asked.'

'Well, *write again*,' said Fanny. 'You never know.'

On principle, Dick was not prepared to reply 'yes' to this. It would be too much like he was following instructions, which he felt would be creating a dangerous precedent. A newly emboldened Fanny might start giving career advice to the others, which would only end in tears.

'They've got my CV on file . . .' he said, rather lamely.

'Hmm,' said Fanny, dissatisfied. 'You always were rather a lazy boy,' she observed suddenly. Dick was a little shocked. She seemed to think she was being droll, however, so he decided to go with it. 'Didn't crawl until you were two; didn't talk until you were three,' Fanny went on. 'Not a Kirrin trait – must be from your mother's side.'

Dick was an incredibly difficult person to rile. He would, in fact, severely inconvenience himself to avoid taking offence at people. However, there were times when one couldn't practically avoid it. And right now, quite frankly, it felt like Aunt Fanny was trolling him. Bring my mother into it, would you? he thought.

Aunt Fanny was still smiling as though she was being funny, so he just nodded and said, 'Hmm.'

'What was I like?' Anne asked.

'Fat,' said Aunt Fanny simply. Anne looked as though she had been connected to the National Grid. 'Very jolly, though, and spoiled by your older brothers. They did love you so much. Oh, look – our food's arrived. How lovely.'

'What was I like?' Julian asked. Aunt Fanny picked up her knife and fork and started getting to grips with the steak and kidney pudding.

'Fanny,' said Julian. 'I was wondering . . .'

She didn't look up, but instead put down her knife and

fork and seasoned her food. Then she picked them up again and took a mouthful. She looked around thoughtfully.

'What I was like,' Julian persisted, the smile on his face faltering, 'when I was a baby? Aunt Fanny!'

'Yes, dear,' she said, looking at him with wondering innocence. He repeated his question.

'I'm so sorry; I'm terribly deaf these days,' she said. 'You do sometimes have to repeat yourself. It's just so loud in here. Yes, please,' she said to the waiter who had come to check their food was okay, and to ask if there was anything she could fetch. 'Could I have a little bit of mustard? Thank you so much. Awful *din* they're making over there,' she tutted. The others looked around the pub, wondering what she was referring to. Then they spotted two Spanish students who were shouting and laughing loudly at the bar, thirty yards away.

They looked at her suspiciously, but she steamed doggedly on with her meal, oblivious. She did not again acknowledge Julian's presence in the room.

It seemed perfectly obvious to Dick that she was avoiding the question because she didn't want to be honest, and the truth was that, when he was a child, Julian had probably been a bit of a pain in the backside. But this possibility clearly did not occur to Julian at all. He looked at her frequently, waiting to have a chance to engage her in conversation, but, as she was serenely ignoring his gaze, the chance did not present itself.

Instead, she spoke exclusively to Anne and George, telling them about a friend of hers who had broken off contact with her daughter over her divorce. 'She doesn't realize that it's the *grandchildren* who'll miss out . . .' she said. Anne and George nodded dumbly at this inexplicable discussion of yet another person who they had never heard of before, wondering what they could possibly say without sounding insincere.

Julian went up to order everyone's desserts, which were presently delivered and eaten, leaving the company in a bulging, semi-comatose silence. Within moments the natural effect of eating a steak and kidney pudding followed by spotted dick with custard took its course, and Aunt Fanny excused herself.

The others looked at each other, wondering who would speak first. Dick decided that for once it would be he who broke the silence.

'Is she feeling quite all right, do you think?' he said. 'I feel as though she's making this . . . a bit . . . hard work . . .'

Anne nodded pensively.

'She seems almost upset about something,' said Julian.

George sighed deeply, and Anne put a hand on her shoulder.

'I'm worried that . . .' she began, and broke off. She struggled with her feelings for a moment and Anne said, 'Ah, darling,' while the men looked away.

George cleared her throat. 'I'm actually worried, for the first time in my life, that I . . . I might actually not *like* her.'

This drew a grave response from the others. They could not think quite what to say.

'Just wait,' Julian said. 'Wait and see. You don't know what might be going on.'

'I did wonder whether she'd had a fight with Daddy,' George said. 'But it doesn't seem very likely – when he's being a git, she usually likes to moan to me about him. But she's not mentioned a word. It's something else. In fact . . .' Stung by having been reduced to an emotional state in front of her cousins, George's temper reappeared.

'I just want you to meet someone nice,' Aunt Fanny said.
'And you won't if you pick your nose like that ...'

'In fact,' she repeated, 'I think she's a bit mean. She just talks about all her friends and relations, and what bad parents they are, and what they get wrong. And, to listen to her, you'd think she says this from a pure spirit of disinterested observation. But it's obvious that she enjoys it, because she does it *aaaaaaall* the time,' said George, drawing the syllable out.

She gulped, and although the others would dearly have liked her to stop, she was just hitting her stride. 'If you leave a pause of just ten seconds, she'll start doing it again. I hate to think I'll end up like that, just a . . . a whistling kettle of resentment.' She seemed to be finished, but a look of menace came into her eyes as she thought of one final point.

'Objectively,' she said, 'she has the trappings of a sophisticated, educated, affluent, charitable, modern Western woman. But take those away and she's no different from the medieval peasant woman, gossiping at the village pump.'

The quality of the silence around her suddenly took on a different air. Instead of listening to her, the others were all just looking exquisitely awkward. It was with a sickening inevitability that George turned to see that, at some point during the preceding speech, her mother had returned from the lavatory.

'I'm feeling rather sleepy after all that food. I think I'll just try and walk it off,' Fanny said, bending down to pick up her bag.

'Mummy,' pleaded George. Her head was swimming.

'No, you all stay here and finish your puddings. That Belgian waffle looks lovely, Julian. What a clever choice. It was lovely to see you all. What a charming place this is. That Irishman looks so peaceful now he's finally fallen asleep. No, no – don't get up. Have a nice afternoon.'

Then she was gone, out onto Charing Cross Road.

CHAPTER NINE

Ungrateful Children

The four separated and went back to their offices. Very little work was done in each case. Very little was said on the WhatsApp group, except a few comments about dinner that evening. There was no point pretending that what had happened had not happened, and George's cousins at least had the insight to know that an unconvincing reassurance is worse than none at all. (George's colleagues, in fact, took her utter glumness as a gift from providence and proceeded about their work for the afternoon, unmolested by her temper.)

They all drifted home that evening at lacklustre speed. They didn't know what to expect when they got there, and they had no overwhelming desire to find out.

George got home first, and it was when she saw that her mother had left and taken her luggage that she finally broke down and cried. She didn't understand how circumstances had led her to do something so awful. She felt appalling, a dreadful person, and truly grief-stricken. And, of course, the one person she wanted to talk to when feeling that way was her mum.

She lay on the sofa and sobbed inconsolably for a good ten minutes, trying to get it out of her system before any of the others came home and saw her this way. Timmy whined and licked her hand, which just made her cry even more.

First home, after her, was Julian. He went to Fanny's room, looked in. Then he came over to where George was sitting at the table and gave her a hug.

'Put the kettle on,' said George. She felt so, so tired – like she had formerly been a person, and was now a used person, ready only for the bin.

'Bugger that,' said Julian. He put a glass in front of her and poured a large measure of whisky.

'I don't like that stuff,' George said.

'I don't care,' said Julian. 'It's medicinal. As your doctor, I recommend you drink it.' He poured an equal measure for himself, then decided it was much too gargantuan for this early in the evening and tried to pour some of it back into the bottle over the sink. Most of it spilt, leading to him swearing violently.

George smiled. She was used to Julian being a blustery leader, oversensitive to criticism. She hadn't been the recipient of his caring-older-brother act before, at least not that she could remember. And his swearing always made her laugh.

'Oh, Satan's ball bag,' Julian muttered, washing the whisky off his hand. 'That stuff was expensive . . .'

'Bit early for that, isn't it?' Dick asked, putting down his rucksack. 'Oh, hi, Anne. You must have been right behind me.'

'Who wants to take Timmy for a walk?' Anne asked.

'Woof!' said Timmy.

They all groggily said yes, and set out into the park. Summer was beginning, the evenings were longer and the park was taking on a pleasing verdant richness, helping them forget the memories of the cold dark walks of winter.

Someone had to broach the subject sooner or later, and it was Julian who eventually asked George how she was going to apologize.

'Oh, God,' said George, sighing. 'Well, it makes

Mother's Day that much more difficult. I'd planned so many nice things.'

'I don't think you should wait *that* long, darling,' said Anne. Her voice carried a tone of reproof and George looked at her sideways. She thought that might be the stupidest remark she'd ever heard.

'Mother's Day is on Sunday,' George said. Simultaneous to this, she felt a sharp clang of pain along her lower jaw, and suddenly realized that there had been a slight twinge in one of her molars for the last few days, which she had been ignoring.

Now it was Anne's turn to look at George as though *she* had gone mad.

'My darling girl, Mother's Day was months ago. What are you talking about?'

'On the calendar!' George protested, rubbing her jaw with her thumb. The pain receded for a moment, then returned, stronger than before. 'The calendar you gave me! Why do you think I circled Mother's Day in red pen like that?'

It was a calendar that Anne had given her on returning from a holiday, last year. George had taped it to the wall over the microwave, to ensure she never lost sight of

'I'm a good mummy to you, aren't I, Timmy?
You'd never treat me like I treat my mum, would you?'
'Woof!'

when Mother's Day was. The boys were looking at her doubtfully too. An awful suspicion was starting to creep into her mind.

'Well, I didn't think about it, to be honest,' said Anne. 'You do all sorts of funny things. Who needs calendars these days, anyway? Just set a reminder on your phone—'

'Wait, wait,' said Julian. 'Can someone explain what the issue is, here?'

'Woof!' said Timmy, returning with the stick. George bent and threw it, and he jogged off again. She was finding it hard to concentrate on the conversation because the pain emanating from her tooth was reminiscent of an air-raid siren.

'Anne's telling me Mother's Day's passed, meaning that, for some reason, the Mother's Day on the calendar she gave me is incorrect. Plus, my bloody tooth is hurting—'

'America,' said Dick.

'What?'

'Oh, George,' said Anne. 'America has a different Mother's Day to Britain. This month's picture is of a man in a cowboy hat, cooking at a barbecue on the edge of the Grand Canyon! Didn't you realize it was American?'

'No!' George roared. 'I was just concentrating on not missing bloody Mother's Day!'

'So you didn't know when British Mother's Day was?' Anne asked.

'Oh, *no one* does,' said George angrily.

'That's true,' said Julian. 'Most people just hear about it a few days before, on the radio, or from a colleague, then sprint to the post office. Fifteen minutes later, they've forgotten about it for another year.'

'Woof!' said Timmy, returning. George threw the stick again.

They walked on in silence and, without a word being spoken, slowly everything became clear. Dick, Anne and Julian were well aware of their culpability in George's failure to give her mother presents on the two previous occasions. Because George had not said anything, it never occurred to them that she was desperate to make this Mother's Day a special one, and partly due to George's own silence, but also due to the donation of the calendar, they had now become complicit in George's failure yet again.

And they now realized that *that* was what had been

up with Aunt Fanny. She was upset, she was hurt, and quite possibly she was doubting her relationship with her daughter – along with these other three ingrates who her daughter lived with, getting this sweet deal on rent, enjoying her hospitality and never expressing the tiniest crumb of gratitude. They started to see how disgustingly smug and arrogant they must seem.

George also realized that Fanny had, of course, been right about going to the dentist all these months. Now George needed to make an emergency appointment, which would cost a bloody bomb.

Dick had decided that it wasn't time to admit to everyone that he had a job interview tomorrow. Being given the talking-to by Aunt Fanny had made him go through his emails. Just to assure himself that he was right, after all, and he *had* emailed the company where he had interned. Of course, he discovered that the email was still in his drafts folder. So he sent it, and within hours received a reply saying what wonderful timing he had, because they had a position going at the moment . . .

George threw the stick for Timmy again.

They walked, and they kicked at clumps of grass, and

they looked at the clouds, and they were for once all silent. Because they were doing what they all instinctively did when faced with a situation where all seemed lost. They were starting to devise a plan. The details were for the moment obscure. But that didn't matter – all they knew was that determination always won through.

And they were now determined to bring off the best Mother's Day present that had ever been presented since the year bloody dot . . .

'Woof!' said Timmy bringing the stick back. George tucked the stick under her arm, then got down on her knees. She kissed his forehead, and rubbed behind his ears.

'I'm a good mummy to you, aren't I, Timmy?'

'Woof!' he agreed.

'You'd never treat me like I treat my mum, would you?'

'*Woof!*' he protested.

'Right answer,' she said, and kissed him again. Then she stood and flung the stick as far as she could.

CHAPTER TEN

An Aunterior Monologue

Aunt Fanny came out of the upholsterer's and hunted in her bag for her keys as she walked down the street towards the car. She always liked visiting Mr Metcalf. He was very reasonable and very good, and always had nice ideas that you wouldn't have thought of yourself. The shop smelt very agreeably of polish and sawdust – although it sometimes also smelt less agreeably of Mr Metcalf.

She got in the car and started it up, and, as she pulled out into the road, became aware of the dull sensation that she was about to have an unhappy thought. What was it? She pulled on to the main road out of Dorchester and rummaged around in her head for it. Oh, yes. That. That, again. Oh, well.

She drove very carefully – politely, almost. She did everything carefully, it seemed, and yet sometimes she wondered where it got her. Her chest felt heavy and she told herself for the thousandth time to avoid the thought. Nothing good could come of it. And if nothing good would come of it, then the thought was best avoided. It wasn't as though she could talk to Quentin about it.

In the old days, she could have spoken to her friend, Mags, but she was gone now. Not dead – just moved to Cornwall, to be near to her son, who had somehow managed to forgive his dreadful wife even after the *third* time she . . .

But Fanny lost interest. When she thought about friends and relations these days, and began to focus on their mistakes, she found she experienced a certain numbness and lost her train of thought.

It was a swooningly beautiful early summer's day in Dorset. The county never looked more handsome than under these conditions. The countryside was proud and lush, and the sun reflected off the distant sea (when she caught sight of it between the hills) like hammered bronze. She took a deep breath, let it out slowly, and tried to relax.

But the monotony of driving soothed her thoughts such

Quentin was lucky not to break his neck,
according to the paramedic.

that, by accident, almost by a process of gravity, they trickled back to the young Kirrins. Fanny signalled for a turn and made her way towards the isthmus, across which lay hers and Quentin's cottage, and, beyond it, Kirrin Island.

Anne was all right, Fanny thought. She lacked ambition, and wanted only a steady, simple life for herself – wanted a husband, in other words. Fanny remembered feeling exactly the same way at her age, and sympathized. After all, not every single woman had to strike out and become a captain of industry. And Anne would have no problem – she was genuinely, stunningly beautiful. Although perhaps a tad prudish.

Julian was a real eyebrow-raiser, to Fanny. Who would be the first person to mention his obvious alcohol problem? He certainly seemed blissfully unaware of it. He was so pompous and touchy, so needy and yet overbearing – a truly horrible combination. No, Fanny had never had much time for him at all.

Dick, however, was her favourite. If she had been a young girl, she knew she would have been interested in him. He was imperturbable, gentle, kind. And handsome, albeit in a modest way. Plus, you could run rings round him intellectually without really trying. A *wonderful* combination.

George . . . well. She had never understood George. It felt, to Fanny, that, when it came to George, she had done her best, and had failed. Parenthood was the one thing where there was no consolation for failure, because a human life was at stake. And yet the only chance one got was the luck of the draw . . .

She forced herself to put an end to these ruminations as she pulled up outside the cottage and applied the handbrake. The fresh sea breeze buffeted her as she got out of the car, and she had to shield her eyes from the brightness reflected off the sea. There were lots of pleasant things about life, and in so very many ways she was incredibly lucky. She smiled (although it was in part owing to the glare of the sunlight) and, going to the front door, let herself in.

'Ahoy-hoy!' she called gaily, using Quentin's preferred method of greeting. The house remained sullenly unresponsive. That was funny. Quentin never went out during the day without telling her first.

She went into the kitchen and picked up the kettle. As she filled it, she saw a note on the kitchen table: a small rectangle of cream-coloured paper with a few words on it. She put the kettle on, then went over and picked it up.

It read, *Go to my study – Q.*

'Hmm,' she said. She looked at the ceiling as she wondered what this betokened. Something odd, for certain. She didn't think Alzheimer's presented in this way, usually, but then Quentin never did anything in a normal way. She took down the teapot as the kettle started to rumble, and then decided that there was no use making tea if she didn't know how many to make it for, and went through to Quentin's study.

Without realising it, she breathed a small sigh of relief that the room was empty, and did not contain an unconscious Quentin. However, there was another note of identical size in the centre of his desk.

Come down to the beach – Q, it said.

'Curiouser and curiouser,' she said, and saw that the French doors leading out of his office towards the edge of the cliff were open, and the curtain flapping. This was most unQuentinlike behaviour. If he wasn't suffering from some form of dementia, then her guess was that he had been kidnapped by spies.

Ho-hum, she thought. Just like the old days.

CHAPTER ELEVEN

On the Beach

She thought about phoning MI-5, but then imagined how the person receiving such a call would react. She dismissed the idea, and instead made her way out and over the grass to the cliff edge. There was a narrow path here, which had always been one to navigate cautiously, even back when she was a teenager. Now, she took it very slowly indeed.

It twisted and turned – it was really only safe for goats, this path down the cliff face. On the way, the beach was hidden by a bluff of rock and only gradually revealed itself over the course of the descent. But, at one turn, Fanny was arrested by an odd sight on the beach below.

The tide was far out, leaving a gorgeous expanse of drying sand, and through this it looked like a child had carved a long, narrow channel, stretching from the cliff towards the sea. It looked like it might, perhaps, be intended for the irrigation of some sandcastle moat. But it was just a line, on its own, extending for thirty feet or more. There was no sign of any other construction – no sandcastle, or anything – to explain it.

Fanny carried on down the trail, taking care with each footstep. It really was a beautiful day, and it was so nice to be out in the fresh air. As long as this nonsense of Quentin's was not especially aggravating, she decided she'd be happy with her lot in life.

Then she turned another corner and saw, far away along the beach, another line in the sand. This one was connected to no form of sand construction either. Fanny began to doubt that it was made by a child at all, and started to wonder what it could be. She did not like mysteries, and hurried as fast as she could along the path, until she turned a corner that took her round the bluff of rock, and a wide swathe of beach was revealed.

She gasped. The two lines she had seen were part of some writing, in letters as wide as a house: they were the letter 'I' and the edge of the letter 'N'. The sentence that revealed itself to her now was:

I NEVER TELL YOU HOW MUCH I LOVE YOU.

How unfortunate, she thought, for the young couple, to have this special moment ruined by the presence of Quentin, with his squint and his belly and his prodigious nose hair.

Fanny cried out with delight. How lovely! So some young man or woman had made this message for their partner. Possibly a proposal of marriage was about to occur – or had already done so. Fanny was beside herself, and now hurried at a frankly unsafe speed along the path.

How unfortunate, she thought, for the young couple, to have this special moment ruined by the presence of Quentin, with his squint and his belly and his prodigious nose hair. Not to mention his mysterious ability to belch loudly at moments of emotional intensity.

It did not occur to her for one moment that the message was from Quentin.

Fanny was nearly at the bottom of the cliff when she saw another line of text had been revealed. Added to the above message were the words, in brackets:

(WHICH IS LOTS AND LOTS)

And then, to one side, in much smaller writing and by another hand (if one could say that writing as tall as a person is by a 'hand'), was a confusing addendum:

Plus, we have beer – Julian.

'Julian?' she said to herself. Then: 'We?' Her romantic

96

vision was fading, but she was not sure what was replacing it. She continued on. Surely the name Julian was a coincidence, she told herself.

Then she saw them, and the breath stopped in her throat.

Julian, Anne, Dick, Timmy . . . and George.

They had set up a picnic on the beach, and George was clearly in charge. There was a hamper, and bottles and glasses, and stones to hold the blanket down, and a cake. There was an air of festivity, over which George (rather than Julian, for once) was presiding.

It finally occurred to Aunt Fanny that this must be an occasion for her sole benefit.

She didn't quite know what to think. Several different feelings hit her at once. A hard and quite painful feeling rose in her throat. It made her eyes water, and she leant against a nearby rock. She felt slightly dizzy, and simultaneously irritated with herself for being so.

She started to wonder whether there was a chance that she had judged them unfairly. And, as quickly as the question was asked, she knew she had. There must be an excuse for what had happened. She suddenly remembered the way they always had been as children – so ardent and fearless and true natured – and she felt guilty for doubting them.

Still, best not to get ahead of herself. Get down there in one piece, say hello. She couldn't wait to see and talk to them again, and for everything from the last few days – and months – to be forgotten.

She was negotiating the final dozen feet of descent when she suddenly stumbled across Quentin, who had clearly been left to wait for her as lookout. He had also, equally clearly, skived off on the job to smoke the pipe that he had promised her he'd given up two years ago. As he caught sight of her, he coughed, said, 'Oh shit,' and slipped off the rock he was standing on, falling ten feet to the beach below.

CHAPTER TWELVE

Ambulance Chasers

Quentin was lucky not to break his neck, according to the paramedic. Although, seeing as he did break his collarbone, he could not be persuaded to see the bright side. Fanny suspected that the pain was not quite as bad as he was making out, and he was just fed up to have been caught smoking, and to have to give it up all over again.

Fanny and the youngsters got into her car and followed along behind the ambulance. The emotional reunion, which had been planned by George in such detail over the course of several days, and worded so carefully, had to be abandoned in exchange for a few minutes of snatched conversation as Fanny negotiated the back lanes towards Dorchester County Hospital.

George was astounded by how readily Fanny accepted all her explanations, as well as her apologies.

'Are you sure, Mummy?' she said. 'Do you believe me?'

'Of course I do,' said Fanny. In truth, she was saddened at herself for ever doubting her daughter's affections, and wanted to put the whole matter behind them. The sequence of events leading to the failed presents did seem *somewhat* implausible, but she did not have the spirit to start questioning details again. She was just happy to be on good terms with her daughter.

'It was a lovely gesture,' she said. 'Really. Thank you, George – and, indeed, a big thank you to all of you.'

'Great,' said Julian, who was trying to open a can of beer as quietly as possible on the back seat.

'Fine,' said Dick, not looking up from his game of Candy Crush.

'Can we always celebrate Mother's Day on the American date from now on,' said George, 'to commemorate this, and never forget it?'

'What, commemorate smashing your dad's shoulder in?' Julian asked, burping and wiping beer from his top lip.

'Yes, I'm sorry about that,' said George. 'Slight administrative hiccup on that front. Still, hopefully they won't actually have to take the arm off.'

'I won't hear a word of apology,' said Fanny, following

the ambulance around a corner. 'My fault entirely. *His* fault, in fact.'

'Mummy,' said George suspiciously. 'Are you happy?'

Aunt Fanny smiled. George looked at her even more suspiciously, and followed her gaze to the ambulance. Then she looked back at her.

'Are you *happy* that this has happened to Daddy?' George asked.

Fanny turned to look at her. She beamed.

'Oh, George,' she said. 'It's the best Mother's Day gift I could possibly have asked for. I've been trying to get Quentin to go for a check-up for years. And he's always refused. It keeps me awake at night – especially when you think what you hear about other men his age. I've been at my wits' end. Now he's in the hospital, I can get them to check on everything: blood pressure, prostate, eyesight, hearing, liver function . . .'

She looked like a new woman. George was astounded. 'I never thought of that. If you'd told me, I could have set about him with a baseball bat years ago. It would have been my sincere pleasure.'

'I can't *tell* you what a relief it is,' said Fanny. 'And,

In truth, she was saddened at herself for ever doubting her daughter's affections, and wanted to put the whole matter behind them.

with him safely in the hospital, I'll be able to give that horrible office a clean without him screaming his head off at me. Change those *ghastly* curtains. And find out what that smell is and get rid of it. Oh, George, you really are the best daughter!'

'Thanks, Mummy,' said George. And then, somewhat diffidently, she added, 'I love you.'

'That's enough of that,' said Julian. 'Any more emotional fulsomeness and I'll be sick all over the back seat. And we don't want that, do we, Timmy?'

'Woof!' said Timmy passionately from the boot. 'Woof, woof!'